JI

J

Hanna-Barbera Authorized Edition

The Flintstones:
DINO GETS A JOB

Story by Horace J. Elias

GREY DAY DAIRY

Rourke Enterprises, Inc.
Windermere, Florida 32786

© 1981 Rourke Enterprises, Inc.
© 1974 Hanna-Barbera Productions, Inc.
First published by Ottenheimer Publishers, Inc.

Published by Rourke Enterprises, Inc., P.O. Box 929, Windermere, Florida 32786. Copyright © 1981 by Rourke Enterprises, Inc. All copyrights reserved. No part of this book may be reproduced in any form without written permission from the publisher. Printed in the United States of America.

Library of Congress Cataloging in Publication Data

Elias, Horace J.
  The Flintstones, Dino gets a job.

  SUMMARY: The Flintstones decide their pet dinosaur should get a job.
  [1. Cave dwellers—Fiction.   2. Dinosaurs—Fiction]   I. Title.   II. Title: Dino gets a job.
PZ7.E395Fi   1981   [Fic]   81-19214
ISBN 0-86592-636-0   AACR2

One evening, Wilma Flintstone said to Fred,
"We simply have to do something about Dino!
He's got to go!"

"Go?" snorted Fred. "Go where? Why?"

"I'll *tell* you why, Fred Flintstone," Wilma said.
"He gets into *everything!* Today he broke my

clothesline and the wash got all muddy. Then, when he was chasing a butterfly, he mashed all the flowers in the garden. After I baked a pie for dinner and left it in the window to cool, he smelled it, stuck up that neck of his, went 'slurp' and that was the end of my pie!"

"Well, what can we do?" asked Fred.

"I have an idea," said Wilma. "Maybe we could get him a job!"

"A job? What kind of a job?" said Fred.

"I'm sure I don't know," answered Wilma. "Why don't we put a notice in the paper and see what happens?"

The next day, this was in the Bedrock Bulletin:

**STRONG, WILLING ANIMAL
WANTS JOB, DOING ANY KIND OF WORK,
SEE ME AT THE FLINTSTONES**

Bright and early the next day, the rockaphone rang. Fred answered, listened for a bit, and said, "Great! Right away!" and hung up.

"Wilma, guess what?" he said. "Dino's got a job!"

Wilma said, "Goodness! That was quick! What kind of a job?"

Fred answered, "The Grey Day Dairy called! Their horse is sick and they want Dino to pull the milk wagon!"

Fred took Dino to the dairy, and Dino went to work.

Everything was fine for a while, but late in the morning the trouble began. The last stop before lunch was to deliver milk to the people who worked at the rock mine.

They stopped at the mine office, so the driver could see how much milk they wanted to buy. He got down from the wagon and started for the office. Just then, Dino caught sight of his father in the distance, who was one of the best rock diggers at the mine. Dino got so excited, he forgot he was hitched to the wagon.

"Daddy! Daddy!" he yelled in dinosaur language, and took off.

He got only a short way before the wagon ran up on a rock and turned over! Dino was so excited he didn't even slow up. The rock mine looked like it had a milk and broken glass blizzard. Wheels and pieces of wagon were scattered all over the place.

They finally caught up with Dino and got him home. About nine o'clock that night they had another call. This time it was from a lady who needed a watchdog because hers had run away.

Fred took Dino to the lady's house and explained to him what he had to do. Then he went home, and he and Wilma went to bed.

The next morning, a strange man brought Dino back.

"What's wrong?" asked Fred. "Where's the lady who hired Dino?"

"She's in the hospital," answered the man.

"Hospital?" asked Fred. "What happened?"

"I live next door to the lady who hired him," said the man. "Everything was fine until the paper boy came by to deliver the paper early this morning. I guess Dino thought he was a burglar, so he roared. The noise was so loud, it sounded like a

mountain falling downstairs! Then he chased the
paper boy up a tree and tried to eat the tree! Here,
he's all yours, and you're welcome to him!''

After the man left, Fred said, "What do we do now?"

At that point, the doorbell rang. Fred went to the door and opened it. Standing there was a man with a round, smiling face, wearing a high silk hat and a long coat.

"I own a circus," he said, "and I saw your notice in the paper. What kind of animal is it?"

"A baby dinosaur! Just what my circus needs!" cried the man. "We'll make a lot of money with him. And pay him, too," he added hastily.

Dino went to work again.

Ten days later, he was back home.

The circus owner said, "It's a shame — we just can't seem to fit him in the right place. We tried him on the tightrope, but he's so heavy, he broke every rope and wire we had. Then we had him doing an act like a trained seal, balancing and

throwing balls with his nose. But he threw the balls so hard, that they made holes in the tent. Finally, we tried him riding a motorcycle through a hoop, but he squashed our motorcycle flat. Sorry, we just can't use him!'' And he went back to his circus.

Wilma said, "What are we going to do, Fred? There doesn't seem to be a job that's right for Dino!"

"I'll tell you, Wilma," answered Fred. "There is one job we know he can do, so I say let him keep right on doing it!"

"What job is that?" asked a puzzled Wilma.
"The job of being a pretty good two-year-old baby dinosaur in this house. He knows all about that, and he's good at it!"

And Pebbles, who was sitting on Dino's back by this time, said "Da Da Goo Goo."

Which meant, "And besides, he's my very best friend!"